Raindrop, Plop!

by Wendy Cheyette Lewison · illustrated by Pam Paparone

SCHOLASTIC INC.
New York Toronto London Auckland Sydney
Mexico City New Delhi Hong Kong Buenos Aires

ONE
little raindrop,
dark, dark sky.

TWO
little raindrops,
clouds go by.

THREE
little raindrops,
splat! splat! splat!

FOUR little raindrops,

boots and hat.

FIVE

little raindrops,
shiny red coat.

SIX
little raindrops,
bright blue boat.

SEVEN little raindrops plop in a cup.

EIGHT
little raindrops,
umbrella up!

NINE little raindrops, puddle fun.

TEN
little raindrops,
still no sun.

Too many raindrops . . .
run! run! run!

**Back in the house now,
that is that!**

**Off with the raincoat!
Off with the hat!**

TEN
little toes
in a nice warm tub.

NINE
soapy bubbles,
scrub-a-dub-dub!

EIGHT
fluffy towels,
soft and white.

SEVEN brass buttons, shiny, bright.

SIX tiny marshmallows
float in a cup.

FIVE
small pretzels.
Gobble them up!

FOUR
furry squirrels
want something to eat.

THREE
hungry birds,
tweet! tweet! tweet!

TWO bright eyes,
what do they see?

Out of the window,
out by the tree?

Raindrops stopping,

ONE

by

ONE.

No more raindrops . . .

SUN! SUN! SUN!

For my husband,
John Lewison,
with love
—W. C. L.

For Rachel
—P. P.

ISBN-13: 978-0-545-01157-0
ISBN-10: 0-545-01157-4

Text copyright © 2004 by Wendy Cheyette Lewison.
Illustrations copyright © 2004 by Pam Paparone.
All rights reserved. Published by Scholastic Inc., 557 Broadway, New York, NY 10012, by arrangement with Viking Children's Books, a division of Penguin Young Readers Group, a member of Penguin Group (USA) Inc.
SCHOLASTIC and associated logos are trademarks and/or registered trademarks of Scholastic Inc.

12 11 10 9 8 7 6 5 4 3 2 1 7 8 9 10 11/0

Printed in the U.S.A. 40

This edition first printing, January 2007

Set in Barbera

Designed by Teresa Kietlinski

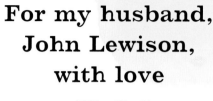